Sneaky

by William S. Yellow Robe, Jr.

No one shall make any changes in this title(s) for the purpose of production. No part of this book may be reproduced, stored in a retrieval system, scanned, uploaded, or transmitted in any form, by any means, now known or yet to be invented, including mechanical, electronic, digital, photocopying, recording, videotaping, or otherwise, without the prior written permission of the publisher. No one shall share this title(s), or any part of this title(s), through any social media or file hosting websites.

For all inquiries regarding motion picture, television, online/digital and other media rights, please contact Concord Theatricals Corp.

MUSIC AND THIRD-PARTY MATERIALS USE NOTE

Licensees are solely responsible for obtaining formal written permission from copyright owners to use copyrighted music and/or other copyrighted third-party materials (e.g. artworks, logos) in the performance of this play and are strongly cautioned to do so. If no such permission is obtained by the licensee, then the licensee must use only original music and materials that the licensee owns and controls. Licensees are solely responsible and liable for clearances of all third-party copyrighted materials, including without limitation music, and shall indemnify the copyright owners of the play(s) and their licensing agent, Concord Theatricals Corp., against any costs, expenses, losses and liabilities arising from the use of such copyrighted third-party materials by licensees. For music, please contact the appropriate music licensing authority in your territory for the rights to any incidental music.

IMPORTANT BILLING AND CREDIT REQUIREMENTS

If you have obtained performance rights to this title, please refer to your licensing agreement for important billing and credit requirements.

Dear Reader:

Please know that this play is published in its raw and unedited form. As such, you may notice elements that could be perceived as typographical or grammatical errors. You may also encounter what seem to be unfinished expressions.

Rather than altering the original work and speculating on Mr. Yellow Robe's authorial intent, we decided to present this play as we found it. We believe this decision best honors Mr. Yellow Robe's creative process and authorial intent while acknowledging that he did not have the opportunity to make final edits.

Should any questions arise as you read or perform this play, please contact us at info@thedgcm.org.

Thank you,

DG Copyright Management, Inc.

SNEAKY received a staged reading at The Public Theater in the spring of 1995. The play was produced twice by the Wakiknabe Theatre Company, once in the fall of 1998 and again at the Taos Arts Association in Taos, NM, in January 1999. Both productions were directed by Rhiana Yazzie.

CHARACTERS

ELDON ROSE – In his early 30s, the middle brother of the family

FRANK ROSE – In his mid-30s, the eldest son

KERMIT ROSE – In his early 30s, the baby of the family

JACK KENCE – A white male in his early 40s, the second generation owner of a funeral home

SETTING

A yard outside the Rose house. Jack Kence's funeral home.
The clearing of meadow.

NOTE ON CASTING

Native characters should always be played by Native actors. The production must know whether the Native actor is an enrolled member of their tribe or of descent, and if they live their life in community as a Native person, before casting. In no instance should someone who claims to be a Native actor but who has no tribal affiliation be cast in one of these roles.

Scene One

(Place: In the yard outside the house.)

(Time: Evening.)

*(The wind is softly blowing. **FRANK** and **ELDON** are by a fire that is slowly burning out. There are a few small boxes around the **BROTHERS**.)*

FRANK. What do you think?

ELDON. I don't know.

    (Pause.)

Yeah. I guess so.

FRANK. We did round everything up?

ELDON. Yeah...yeah. I did.

    (Pause.)

What about the old blue steamer trunk?

FRANK. I found it in the root cellar.

ELDON. Too bad. Hey, what about those boxes of sewing patterns? Them too?

FRANK. Yeah. I got them, too.

ELDON. The pictures?

FRANK. Not all of them.

ELDON. Good.

FRANK. I kept some of them. Here, take a look.

>   (**FRANK** *removes a small cigar box from a bigger box and hands it to* **ELDON**. **ELDON** *eagerly goes through it.*)

She doesn't want anyone to have these. Burn them when you're done.

ELDON. The Smithsonians would want these…and this one, and that one – damn! You think we did right?

FRANK. Yeah, just like when the old man passed away. Did the same thing, but at a different spot.

>   (**FRANK** *takes a bible from a box, and* **ELDON** *spots it.*)

I guess we could…

ELDON. Don't throw the Bible on the fire, Frank! Jesus.

>   (**ELDON** *takes the bible.*)

Hey – you remember? Colleen Hammer came driving up and tried to get the old man's rifle – the octagon .22?

FRANK. Yeah. The way she came driving up with all those wooden apple boxes in the back of her old white Ford. Her small, squinty eyes looking around the place. And that greasy apron she wears, black spots on her dress.

>   (**FRANK** *laughs.*)

We used to tease you about her. We told you she was your bride, picked out for you.

ELDON. Quit teasing me like that. No way. Not that bad. Oh yeah, oh yeah. She said her "cuzin" let her have the rifle. And all the time it was burning with the rest of Dad's stuff. I thought she was going to scream when you told her if she wanted it, to go and get it. The fire had melted the barrel into a U shape.

(Pause.)

Where is Colleen now, I wonder? I thought she would show up by now.

FRANK. Probably mad about something.

ELDON. Mad? What for? Because of the...

FRANK. You didn't marry her.

ELDON. Damn you, Frank. You're always...

FRANK. I'm just kidding you, Eldon. It's too early yet. The news hasn't gotten around. When the word does, she'll be stopping by. She'll come in that old Ford. Probably with a bunch of cardboard boxes in her trunk and plenty of her grandchildren to help her with her haul.

> *(***KERMIT*** enters. He is singing and carries a small paper sack. He sets the sack near the porch, takes a bottle from the sack and drinks, then he sets the bottle down and goes to the fire.)*

It'll be just a matter of time. She'll come waddling into the yard like a fat duck to water. I don't like...hey!

(Pause.)

Kermit? Why don't you go into the house and stretch out?

KERMIT. Ma?

ELDON. Oh Christ...yeah! Kermit, you look tired.

> *(Turns his back.)*

KERMIT. Momma? Oh...momma...

> *(Stands at the fire.)*

FRANK. Come on, Kermit. You need the rest.

> *(Grabs ***KERMIT****'s arm.)*

FRANK. Let's go.

> *(He starts to lead **KERMIT**, but **KERMIT** breaks free and staggers.)*

KERMIT. No...no! I can do it by myself.

ELDON. Hey, ringy! He's only trying to help you.

KERMIT. I can do it... I can do it! Fuck!

> *(He mumbles, staggers to the porch, and sits, then takes out the bottle and drinks. **FRANK** watches as **ELDON** lifts some of the pictures from the box and sticks them inside his shirt.)*

ELDON. How is he? Is he going to get real ringy on us? *(Softly.)* Frank? Frank?

FRANK. Speak up! He'll be all right.

ELDON. Are you sure?

KERMIT. Yeah! Don't lose any sleep, El. I'm not going to die. I can hear you, even though I don't want to... goddamn it! Paw-uk-nah-uk!

ELDON. Was he cussing at me again? Huh? I hate it when he cusses at me in Assiniboine.

FRANK. Don't worry, it's only drunk talk. Hey – but you'll have one hell of a hangover tomorrow.

> *(No reply from the **BROTHERS**.)*

Christ. I remember drinking with him four years ago. He met me on a Friday night at the Long Horn. Denise took the kids and her mother to bingo.

> *(**KERMIT** gets up and walks over to the **BROTHERS**, trying to hide the bottle on his way over.)*

KERMIT. You bet, partner! What yah guys doing?

FRANK. I wasn't planning anything. Then I started drinking shots of whiskey and had a beer chaser. Glad people told me, otherwise I would've forgotten. Anyways, he came over and sat with me. And then it was park-the-car time. What was it you were drinking?

KERMIT. Top secret – mustn't tell. It was muscatel.

(He laughs and offers **FRANK** *a drink on the side.)*

FRANK. No thanks. When the Long Horn closed we got two cases of beer and a jug of wine and went to a house party – it was a house, anyway. We finished the beer and wine and I passed out.

KERMIT. Wussed out.

FRANK. Saturday afternoon we woke up, hot and sweaty, in the truck. Bought another case of beer and went to – Clem's bar, I think? Yeah. And we drank until Clem's closed. We drove around and finished off the case. I quit drinking Sunday, and I think this guy went drinking until next Sunday.

KERMIT. Hey, hey, hey, Frank. You wussed out on me.

ELDON. See! This is what I mean.

KERMIT. Oh shit. You mad? Fuck! Good time, huh Frank?

(Pats **FRANK** *on the back and looks at* **ELDON.** *He goes back to the porch.)*

My brother.

ELDON. Now that Mom is dead he'll...

FRANK. No, no...it's up to him. One way or another, he'll decide for himself like I did.

ELDON. Are we going to have a feast after the funeral?

FRANK. Yeah. Claire said she would do it. The kids will help. Aunty Babs, Joan, and Ava said they would help, too.

ELDON. When are we going to have the funeral?

FRANK. Wednesday.

ELDON. Why Wednesday? Hell that's a four-day wait. Hell that's two days after we're supposed to have the feast!

FRANK. I know.

ELDON. Kence just wants it on Wednesday 'cause he can make more money. Keeping her in storage like a piece of furniture.

FRANK. He's the only mortician in a hundred miles. Hell – I don't like him, but he's the only one nearby.

(Pause.)

Hey!

ELDON. What?

FRANK. Why don't we bury Mom ourselves?

ELDON. You mean, let Kence prepare the body and we dig the hole?

FRANK. I've been thinking. We don't need to put all those chemicals and preservatives in her body. Why preserve her dead body like she was a damn beet?

ELDON. I don't know, Frank...

FRANK. Well, I sure the hell do.

ELDON. Yeah, but Father Crane will be pissed if he doesn't get to pray over her.

FRANK. To hell with Crane. He was there when she died. He had a chance to sprinkle his water on her and pray over her.

ELDON. If you think about it that way...

FRANK. Remember when I used to work for Kence Senior? He told me the secret for funerals, El. You want to know what they are? One – you need a dead body.

Two – a hole in the ground. Three – transportation to get the body to the hole in the ground. Four – start a bank account.

ELDON. No...uh – uh...no...no...

FRANK. Don't worry, I'll take care of you.

(*Pause.*)

We have a right to do this. Even Kermit.

ELDON. Not that drunk.

FRANK. We're all family.

ELDON. But what about Dad's relatives?

FRANK. We did right by Dad – they'll think we did the same with Mom. We have to stick together and ride this one out. The others – they'll figure it out.

ELDON. Frank... Frank...

(*Pause.*)

You're just... You're really serious about this?

FRANK. Damn right I am.

ELDON. I thought you were just joking.

FRANK. No. And I'm not doing it because I'm trying to get out of Kence's fee. We'll give him his money when we're finished. I want us to bury her. Not a stranger and with his strange ways.

ELDON. How will we do it?

FRANK. She's always talked about being buried in the traditional way, remember?

ELDON. Yeah? Where are we going to start shoveling?

FRANK. Nooo... Eldon, no – not their way, our traditional way. Not buried in the ground. Bury her with the wind, in a tree.

ELDON. What about her decaying smell, in the wind?

FRANK. If you're worried about the smell, we can burn the body after the funeral. Just like in the old days, no one will find it. We can find an old tree and place wood around it and set them on fire.

ELDON. Then, why don't we just have her cremated? I'll pay for part of the cost.

FRANK. You're not listening. It isn't the money that's important. Way back when, it was the responsibility of the family to bury their own.

ELDON. That was a long time ago. Two or three hundred years ago. It wasn't right, remember?

FRANK. For who, Eldon? Us? Eldon – this way, her grave won't be disturbed. They uncover a bunch of unmarked graves and take the bodies out and in a few more years, who knows? Some scientist will come along and discover Mom's body and take it off to some college or university. Her skull sitting on a little wood box under glass. Her bones sawed up, spine and all, like beef ribs. Then they'll put them under a microscope. Is that right? I sure the hell don't think so. And I'm not going to allow it to happen.

(Pause.)

Goddamn it, El.

ELDON. Well, do you really know how to bury her in the traditional way? I don't recall having heard of anybody doing it recently. I don't know of anyone who has done it or remembers seeing it. And if nobody knows how to do it, I don't want to mess with it.

FRANK. You don't, huh? I remember Grandma telling us how they used to do it. And I remember a little of what Grandpa told me.

ELDON. Yeah? But do you know enough about it so we can do it right?

FRANK. Grandma told me how to do it. And I know she told it to you and Kermit when she used to babysit us. If we try to do it right, and do – do it right, we'll tell our kids about it. And they'll tell their kids. We can keep it going just like Grandpa and Grandma did with us.

ELDON. But what about the law? Her will? And if we're not caught by the cops, we still have Kence to settle with. And I don't want to mess with that guy.

FRANK. I've seen the will.

ELDON. How did you see it?

FRANK. In her last couple of weeks, she called me to her house and asked me to be with her. That's when she made her will out. Kence was there, too.

ELDON. Why didn't Mom call me?

FRANK. I don't know. Mom probably didn't want to bother you.

ELDON. I would have come if somebody would have told me. They call me for everything else. Christ! What the hell was Kence doing there? I'm her own son.

FRANK. Anyway – in her will she was going to request to be buried near the place she grew up at. She wanted to be buried in the traditional way. And Kence told her it wasn't possible. He knew where she wanted to be buried at, but he didn't know how to perform the ceremony. And he suggested she go with the American traditional funeral, everybody else does.

    (Pause.)

ELDON. Well, why didn't you say something then, Frank? Huh?

FRANK. Not in front of Kence. He would've really put the blocks to us before we even had a chance.

ELDON. It just doesn't seem right. We could get caught.

FRANK. Who's going to know, huh?

ELDON. Someone will see us and tell. Maybe one of Mom's friends...

FRANK. They won't tell. I'll explain it to them. I'll put the will in the tribal newspaper if you want me to. Will and all. El, Mom didn't like the white man's funeral. She said all it had to do with is money, and nothing else. You can't even cry without the priest's permission.

(**KERMIT** *slowly staggers to them.*)

If you decide no, we can't do it. You're the second to the oldest.

ELDON. If you can't do without me... I'm a member of the family now, huh? Okay, I'll go along with you, but we have to keep this to ourselves. I don't want this going through the moccasin telegraph.

FRANK. It'll go through the moccasin telegraph. By the time it gets around the rez, it'll be too late for Kence and the cops to do anything.

ELDON. It sounds slick and all. I...

KERMIT. What's up?

(*Tries to place his hand on* **FRANK**'*s shoulder.*)

FRANK. Kermit. We've decided to bury Mom ourselves. What do you think?

KERMIT. E-chaw-wok-nok! Hell, yes! Let's do-er!

(*He nearly walks into the fire, but is saved by* **FRANK.**)

ELDON. Chh... Christ! He's not even in walking condition. Frank, if we get caught it'll be because of him. He's lost his mud. He hasn't cared about Mom. He's lived off of her. Now he wants to help us steal her from the morgue, because you've come up with this idea.

KERMIT. What? Steal Momma?

FRANK. Hold on now, Eldon. He has the right to be a part of this too. You wouldn't like to bury Mom by yourself?

KERMIT. Yeah, you tight-ass human.

ELDON. Shut up!

FRANK. I want us to do the burying, because that's the way we've always done things. By ourselves – family. We didn't get to bury Dad, but now we've got a chance to bury Mom as a family.

KERMIT. What's this shit about stealing Momma?

FRANK. We're going to take Mom from the mortician and bury her ourselves. Are you in?

KERMIT. Shit – yeah!

(*He falls and* **FRANK** *tries to catch him.*)

ELDON. Oh, goddamn it!

FRANK. Don't be afraid of Jack Kence. I'll handle him.

ELDON. Like you did at Mom's will? I'm not afraid of him. Who said I was?

KERMIT. Fuck you. You're afraid of him because he has money. I'm not. I'm like Frank.

ELDON. Shut up, you drunk.

(*He goes to* **KERMIT** *and pushes him.*)

FRANK. Easy, Eldon. I know Kence has money and a lot of connections, but he also has our mother.

KERMIT. Yeah. Who we talking about again?

FRANK. We're going to get her back. When Mom died, no one asked me what I wanted. Kence just came in and took her without permission.

ELDON. Yes, but he has a right, Frank. He's a mortician. The county coroner. It's his job.

FRANK. It's our job, Eldon. And the thing is, we don't get paid for doing it.

KERMIT. That's right. We can't let the son of a bitch do our job for us.

ELDON. What if he calls the cops on us? Huh? Or even the FBI? We could be up shit creek without a paddle. And if we go to jail? Hell, the pen? What happens to my family?

KERMIT. They'll be better off.

ELDON. Shut up, Kermit! You don't have a wife and kids to worry about. I do. And you have kids, too, Frank. What happens to them? How are we going to support them from prison?

FRANK. We won't get caught, El. Your problem is you're always thinking like one of them. So what if Kence has connections with the cops? That's the risk we have to take.

ELDON. Okay.

KERMIT. You're damned right. I'm behind you one hundred percent.

> *(He goes into a fast grass dance, does a few steps, and nearly falls over into the fire but is saved by* **FRANK.***)*

FRANK. We're not cooking fry bread. If you bum yourself up, you aren't going to be worth a shit to us.

ELDON. You're not as it is now.

KERMIT. Sure I am. I can keep watch for you two guys. No problem.

FRANK. Okay. Let's get started.

ELDON. What about the fire.

> (**ELDON** *picks up some of the boxes and turns his back to the* **BROTHERS**.)

FRANK. We'll shovel dirt on it.

> (**ELDON** *walks off.*)

ELDON. One big chief and a damn drunken Indian.

FRANK. What?

KERMIT. Damn right.

> (**KERMIT** *attacks the fire, and* **FRANK** *helps him toss dirt onto it. Blackout.*)

Scene Two

(Place: Jack Kence's funeral home.)

(Time: Late at night, same day.)

*(**FRANK** and **ELDON** hide behind and run to several objects before they reach the funeral home. They enter the funeral home, and **FRANK** leads **ELDON** to the surgical room. **KERMIT** slowly follows his brothers. Two slabs are in the middle of the room with a surgical tray at the side of each slab, and a large sink on one side of the wall. The other wall is lined with glass and wood cabinets, each cabinet containing surgical equipment. Bodies lie on each slab. The **BROTHERS** are carrying flashlights.)*

ELDON. God, it smells funny in here. What is that smell, Frank?

FRANK. Death and all its causes.

*(**ELDON**'s light shines on the bodies.)*

ELDON. Hey! There are two of them. How do we know which one of them is Mom?

FRANK. You do the one on the right and I'll do the left.

*(**KERMIT** enters the room. He is humming the theme song from a popular spy series.* The two **BROTHERS** go to the bodies. **KERMIT** goes to **ELDON**. **FRANK** is the first in pulling back the sheet.)*

I found her. I found Mom.

(**ELDON** *pulls back the sheet and looks at* **FRANK**. **FRANK** *shakes his head "no," then* **ELDON** *looks at the body.*)

ELDON. Ohhh...my god...

KERMIT. What's up, El? Can't handle it, eh?

(**ELDON** *shows* **KERMIT** *the body, and they become sick.*)

Ohhhh...

FRANK. Hold on. Hang on to it.

(**ELDON** *gets sick.* **FRANK** *grabs* **ELDON** *and* **KERMIT**, *and takes them to the sink.* **FRANK** *goes back to the slab and examines the body. He finds a foot tag.*)

Jesus. It's Uncle Joe Yellow Foote, and half his face is gone.

(**KERMIT** *and* **ELDON** *take turns vomiting into the sink.* **FRANK** *reads the foot tag.*)

Accident victim: Hit and run. Identification: Joseph Alvin Yellow Foote, Senior. Occupation: Vagrant.

ELDON. God – it made me sick. Let's get the body and go.

FRANK. You're right, Eldon. Kermit? Can you make it back to the pickup by yourself?

KERMIT. Who, who – who hit me?

(*He is on his hands and knees rocking back and forth. Slobber dangles from his mouth and touches the floor. He slumps to the floor.*)

Son of a bitch! Who hit me, goddamn it! Come on! I'll take you all on...

FRANK. Better help him out to the truck, El. He won't make it by himself.

ELDON. Frank! I can't! Are you going to carry Mom by yourself?

FRANK. No. But he needs help – now!

KERMIT. Float like a butterfly, sing like a bee-grasshopper.

ELDON. We'll get caught. I know it.

FRANK. El, listen to me. You help Kermit back to the truck and I'll clean up this mess. Then come back and help me.

*(**FRANK** walks back to **KERMIT** and helps him to his feet.)*

KERMIT. Bring them on – bring them all on...

ELDON. All right, all right. I'll do it.

KERMIT. Frank... Frank? Oh, there you are. We'll take them all on...

FRANK. Right, Kermit.

*(**ELDON** and **KERMIT** begin to walk out the door.)*

KERMIT. Oh – Christ! Momma!

FRANK. Hurry up, El. Just do it and be sure to come back and help me.

KERMIT. Hey, you guys. Bathroom. Guys – bathroom!

*(**ELDON** finds a place to grab **KERMIT** and leads him out the door. **FRANK** starts a search for paper towels. He finds them and wets them in the sink, then he starts to wipe the floor where **KERMIT** was and then the sink. He looks for a garbage can and finds one, but it is filled. He steps on the pedal of another can, and the lid opens. **FRANK** crams the paper towels into the can, a disposal can for dead organ and tissue. **FRANK** nearly vomits. He washes his hands and is faced again with*

the task of disposing of the paper towels. He wads them up and puts them in his shirt pocket, glances around the room and does a quick go-over of it, checks the floor and then the two slabs. He goes over to his mother and gently removes the blanket from her face.)

FRANK. Ma, I don't... I don't know if I can live without you. You've always given me your support. Helped me out when I needed it. My whole family loves you. We're all going to miss you.

(**ELDON** *enters. He stops and watches.*)

You've worked hard all your life, Mom. And now you suffer no pain. Thank you for being our mother. It'll be really tough without you in this world. We'll try. And we'll always remember you. Damn. I don't know if I can carry this whole family, Mom. Please help me find a way to do it – or to let go.

(Pause.)

We should all be going and just let go.

ELDON. Frank? Frank?

FRANK. Goodbye, Uncle Joe... What is it?

ELDON. There's a security cop. Are you all right?

FRANK. Yeah.

ELDON. Well, there's a security cop. I thought he saw me and Kermit, so I headed down the alley.

FRANK. Where's Kermit?

ELDON. I put him in a garbage bin. We'll get him later.

FRANK. Damn.

ELDON. He'll be all right. He doesn't even know what's going on. When I put him in, he gave me his wallet. Let's get Mom.

(They both go to the body and pick it up. A light shines under the door.)

FRANK. Oh-oh! Someone's coming, El.

ELDON. You take her.

*(He drops his end of the body. **FRANK** hangs onto his end.)*

FRANK. What the hell are you doing, El? Just pick her up, and we'll take her and put her back on the slab and hide.

*(They do, then hide, **FRANK** behind a cabinet and **ELDON** alongside of Joe, covering himself with Joe's blanket. The door opens, and a ray of light sweeps the room. The light stops and the door closes.)*

El? El? I think it's okay. Let's go. Where are you?

ELDON. Oh...man.

*(He climbs out from under the sheet. **FRANK** crosses to him.)*

FRANK. Don't feel bad. I would have done the same thing.

ELDON. I feel like one of those microwave sandwiches. Okay – I'm sorry I dropped Mom. I want to go now. I don't want to hang around here.

FRANK. You're not the only one. We'll have to wait a bit.

ELDON. Why? The guard is gone. Don't know why you'd need a guard at a funeral home anyway.

FRANK. Somebody might steal something.

ELDON. Oh, Christ.

FRANK. Really. There are a lot of expensive things around here. When I was working here, somebody stole some clothes.

ELDON. Clothes?

FRANK. Yeah. Kence has clothes that zip up in the back. It makes it easier for him to dress the body.

ELDON. Who stole them?

FRANK. Remember that one year all the winos around town looked real sharp?

ELDON. Jesus. How could they? Let's go.

(**FRANK** *goes to the door and looks out.* **ELDON** *sniffs himself.*)

FRANK. It looks okay, but let's wait for a bit more. He was probably making his rounds.

(*Crosses to* **ELDON**.)

ELDON. Do I stink?

FRANK. Sometimes – that's why I always stand left of you. Nah, but not now. You're okay.

ELDON. Okay, but I want to get cleaned up before we have the funeral and get a star quilt. We're not going to bury Mom in this.

FRANK. (*Crosses to the door and checks.*) All right.

(*Crosses back to* **ELDON**.)

It's okay. Ready?

(*Picks up one end of the body and* **ELDON** *picks up the other.*)

ELDON. Frank? Are you scared?

FRANK. Yeah. Let's take Mom and make some tracks.

(*They carry the body out, stopping on the way to pick up* **KERMIT**. *They carry* **KERMIT** *and the mother in the blanket. Blackout.*)

Scene Three

(Place: Five miles from town, near the river and a clearing of a meadow.)

(Time: Early in the morning, next day.)

*(There is a human mound – **KERMIT** and the body. **KERMIT** stirs and rolls off the body, rolls near a small fire, and shakes a little from the morning cold. Then he reaches out to wrap a blanket around himself. The blanket isn't there. He slowly wakes up. He rests himself on his elbows and tries to refocus his eyes. He sees his mother with her blanket.)*

KERMIT. Damn, it's chilly.

(Pause.)

Did you go to the softball tournament, too? I didn't see you. You probably seen me.

(No reply.)

I sure am cold...and lonesome.

(Leans towards her.)

You know, hey? You know, you have a blanket. And I don't have any. Brr... And I suppose you're cold, too.

(He touches her.)

Damn...damn! You're really cold...freezing.

(Touches himself.)

Hey! Hey there, partner. I tell you what. You share your blanket with me. I'll be good.

(No reply.)

Don't worry. Don't worry, honey. I won't hurt you even if you don't want to share your blanket.

(No reply.)

Don't be stuck up. I'll even let you sleep near the fire. Be, be – be sure you don't burn yourself from the sparks.

*(No reply. **KERMIT** begins to pull at the blanket.)*

Don't be a tight ass. Corne on baby. Share with me.

*(**ELDON** and **FRANK** enter.)*

Baby...darlin'. Baby cakes?

ELDON. After I showered up – I guess the cops called while I was showering, and my wife told them I was sleeping, and...

KERMIT. Oh, baby. Ohhh...baby, baby, sweet baby cakes...

(He caresses his mother's shoulder.)

ELDON. What the hell is he doing? I thought he was passed out.

FRANK. How the hell do I know.

KERMIT. Yeah. Ohhh...baby...

(He uses his other hand to caress his mother.)

ELDON. Oh shit!

*(Runs over and kicks **KERMIT** away.)*

KERMIT. Ow! Fuck!

ELDON. Frank, did you see what he was doing?

FRANK. Yeah. Kinda hard to miss it, El.

KERMIT. I wasn't doing anything wrong. Fuck. I was doing it with love.

ELDON. I thought you said if we left him alone, passed out, he wouldn't do anything.

FRANK. I was wrong.

ELDON. Do something then, Frank!

FRANK. What? What do you want me to do, Eldon?

KERMIT. It's just a girl. Christ. Eldon fucking freaks out on everything. Shit!

ELDON. A girl? You don't know, do you? Frank – he doesn't even know.

FRANK. He's been drinking, Eldon. He just must be coming out of it.

ELDON. All right, Frank. A girl, huh? Come here.

*(Grabs **KERMIT** and pulls him near their mother's face.)*

It's Mom, Kermit. It's your mother.

*(**KERMIT** looks at the face.)*

FRANK. Kermit?

KERMIT. Oh, god damn...

(He crawls away from the body and scratches the ground.)

Damn...damn...it...

ELDON. I had to, Frank. And you, Frank – you are going to have to stop taking care of him. You bought him that wine tonight. He has to live down whatever he does.

KERMIT. Keep away from me.

FRANK. Come on, you guys. Knock it off.

KERMIT. Why the hell did you guys have to do that, huh?

ELDON. Because you are a drunk. You can't be blaming what you do on being drunk all the time, Kermit. I don't want my little brother to be a drunk.

KERMIT. Yeah? Well, you're an apple, red on the outside. Hell! You're white all over, in and out. You're a white man. We should cut you out.

ELDON. What? No, I'm your brother.

FRANK. Don't say any more, you two.

KERMIT. You know what Mom used to say, Eldon? Huh? She used to say how she raised two Indin sons and one businessman.

ELDON. That's a lie.

KERMIT. Don't believe me? Ask Frank. She said one loves celebrations, one loves hunting and building things, and the other one loves money.

ELDON. She didn't mean it that way, Kermit. That's not true.

KERMIT. You're a white man, Eldon. I hate to see one of my older brothers turn into a white man. You dress like Jack Kence – you even smell like him.

ELDON. Stop it, Kermit.

KERMIT. Mr. Chamber of Commerce. Only Indin there. Yeah. And you're such a big wheel. You and your stink smoke shack. Indins around here are laughing at you behind your back.

ELDON. I don't give a shit about that.

KERMIT. That's probably why you wanted all of Mom's things. So you could sell them at your smoke shack.

ELDON. No, it was for my girls. They deserve...

KERMIT. Mr. Businessman. Last Thanksgiving, when you put that big cardboard cut of a turkey around your smoke shack, the stink little trailer. No one else, but you. Ohhh…shit! All the places I've been. All the Indin people I know. You're the only one who celebrates Thanksgiving, the coming of the white man. But then again, it's like welcoming your brothers, enit? You break your ass recognizing them, but you sure as shit can't recognize me when you see me on the streets, can you?

ELDON. I've always come to help.

FRANK. Don't be talking about these things now, Kermit.

KERMIT. Why not? Now's a good time as any. He'll leave and forget all about us. Ignore us when he sees us, because we're Indins and he's not.

ELDON. I only ignored you one time, Kermit! One time! And that's because you were sitting on the steps of the Sherman Hotel. You've probably forgotten that… I bet you don't even remember. You had puked all over yourself and didn't know it. Peed your pants, your hair was greasy and matted, and you didn't even know it. You were bumming people who were coming and going into the hotel. You were mumbling away. "Help me, help me." The cops wanted to take you in. They stopped at the smoke shack and told me, but I talked with them, promised them I would come and get you.

 (Pause.)

And when I pulled up and parked my car, you were mumbling away, "Eldon, Eldon." I walked over to you, and you didn't even hear me when I called your name. You didn't even recognize my voice. You didn't even recognize me, period! You just kept on mumbling. I felt so bad for you. I picked you up and took you to my house and cleaned you up. And then, I…I cried. Ever since that time I told myself – I promised myself

– if I ever saw you drunk like that again, I wouldn't recognize you. It would be easier for me if you were some other wino, but you're my brother.

(Pause.)

It is true, Kermit. I didn't recognize you. And there were times I didn't want to recognize Frank and Dad. All three of you were drunk. I'm a member of the family now, huh? You know what – what hurts me the most? You all three treated me like another drunk, not like a brother. Just because I didn't drink with you guys didn't mean I was too good for you guys. It just meant I was sober.

(Pause.)

The next time, Kermit...I will disown you.

KERMIT. See, see! Too fucking good!

FRANK. I would've done the same thing, Kermit.

KERMIT. No you wouldn't – no, Frank. You're my brother. Not like this guy.

ELDON. Damn you.

*(Charges **KERMIT**.)*

FRANK. Don't, Eldon.

KERMIT. You want to fight, huh? I'll kick your fucking ass. Come on. You and the big son of a bitch, Frank. Both of you, come on!

FRANK. Knock it off, Kermit!

KERMIT. You're not so fucking good as you act, Frank.

FRANK. Shut up, Kermit!

KERMIT. But first I'm going to knock the shit out of this bastard. Yeah. You're both alike.

FRANK. You'd better settle down.

KERMIT. I don't have to. Damn it! Come on and fight!

(*He slaps* **ELDON**. **ELDON** *doesn't do anything.* **KERMIT** *tries to dance around like a boxer. He tries to slap* **ELDON** *again, but* **ELDON** *grabs his arm and pulls* **KERMIT** *to him and holds him.* **KERMIT** *tries to break free.*)

Damn you! You fucking ass! Let me go! I can take care of...of myself.

(**KERMIT** *stops struggling.* **ELDON** *loosens his hold. There is the sound of a car.* **FRANK** *crosses to his* **BROTHERS** *and touches them. The sound of the car becomes louder.*)

ELDON. What?

FRANK. Listen. I think it's a car.

ELDON. Maybe it's just a farmer.

FRANK. Too early. Did you close the gate?

ELDON. I think so.

FRANK. You'd better go check and see.

(**ELDON** *begins to exit.*)

Wait. We don't have time.

ELDON. What do we do?

FRANK. We have to hide Mom.

ELDON. Let's cover her up.

(*They cover her with the blanket.*)

FRANK. It won't work.

ELDON. What if one of us lies down and pretends we're sleeping

(*They look at* **KERMIT**.)

KERMIT. Oh, no, no!

FRANK. Come on, Kermit. You have to. Just this one time.

ELDON. If you do it, we don't have to come up with a good excuse...

KERMIT. No – ah, shit...

(*He starts to get to his knees.* **ELDON** *removes the blanket from their mother's body.* **KERMIT** *lies on top of their mother and they cover them.* **JACK KENCE** *enters.*)

FRANK. Be quiet, Kermit.

JACK. Good morning.

FRANK. Hello, Jack.

ELDON. Uh...hi, Jack.

JACK. Goddamn, it's chilly this morning. What're you boys doing out here so early?

ELDON. We – we're gathering a few things for the feast. You know, tea, meat, cheese...

JACK. Well, you guys shouldn't be spotlighting. It's illegal. Hard to do without any rifles.

ELDON. Jack...that's because we're not allowed to use rifles, traditionally. We use our cars.

JACK. Uh-huh.

FRANK. Calm down, Eldon. What're you doing here Jack?

JACK. I have one hell of a mess on my hands, Frank. You see, I got a phone call from my security man. It's kind of embarrassing. He said Elva Rose's body is missing.

ELDON. No!

JACK. Yes – said he saw your pickup outside of my place last night. Well, I kinda figured you might know where your mom's body is at.

ELDON. By golly, we don't know what the hell you're talking about, Jack.

JACK. Oh. I see. What's this over here?

ELDON. It's our baby brother. He's asleep.

JACK. Well, what's he laying on?

ELDON. Traditionally – straw.

> (*Crosses to the body.*)

JACK. Let's take a look.

ELDON. Oh shit. Oh shit.

> (**ELDON** *begins to take off but is stopped by* **FRANK**.*)*

JACK. Kermit, come on kid. Get up.

> (**ELDON** *crosses over to* **JACK** *and stops him from touching the blanket.*)

ELDON. I said, it's our baby brother Jack.

JACK. But this blanket is familiar.

> (*Pulls on the blanket and then* **KERMIT**.*)*

Get up, kid.

> (*Rolls* **KERMIT** *off the body.*)

Oh, Christ. Have you guys lost your marbles?

> (**JACK** *examines the body.*)

Didn't really damage anything.

ELDON. Sorry, Jack…

JACK. Sorry, shit! Eldon. Help me take this back to my car.

FRANK. Take your hands off our mother, Jack.

JACK. Look, this is getting really sick. Now help me take your mother back to my place, and we'll forget all about this. Eldon?

ELDON. I can't.

JACK. Why not?

KERMIT. Why should he? You're just a white man.

JACK. Look, I know this is a difficult time, but I have a job to do. Now help me out and we can all go home and forget this happened. I'm not in a great mood, guys. I don't want to be out here all damn morning long. Let's go.

> *(No response.)*

Frank, be reasonable. All right. Eldon, give me hand here? I'm taking this body back with me.

> *(No response.)*

You fellas don't seem to understand this. We seem to have a hell of time communicating like normal people. She belongs to me – mine – and I still have a lot of work to do. I have to do some more preparations, dress her up, and I have a backup at the home and the sooner I can get this one done, I can move on. Now come on, El.

ELDON. I can't, Jack. My brothers and I have decided she's going to stay with us.

JACK. What?

FRANK. That's right, Jack. Our mother is staying with us.

JACK. All the times you worked with my father, Frank. I thought you were more reasonable than this.

FRANK. I am, Jack.

JACK. Not as far as I can see.

KERMIT. Then you must be blind and white.

JACK. Be quiet, kid. You guys can get into a lot of trouble for this. I'm not joking. I'd hate to see it happen.

FRANK. That's the chance we're willing to take.

JACK. I came here without notifying the police where I am. The cops, both tribal and white, are patrolling all around town and the surrounding area looking for your mother.

KERMIT. Did you tell them what she was wearing, hey?

JACK. Kermit, I've always heard you were a little drunken smart ass, but I didn't think it was this bad. Goddamn. If you guys don't give me some damn good reasons in the next few minutes, I'll have to go back to my car and call the cops out here. You can save us all a lot of trouble if you can give me a hand and take your mother's body back to my car, and I'll take it back with me.

KERMIT. Do it yourself. We don't work for you.

JACK. You know, Eldon, I remember a young man coming up, working very hard to succeed in business. Then making it. Becoming a member – the first Indian, mind you – to make the chamber of commerce. Now, to lose it all on one bad move... I know you must have had one hell of a battle with the bottle...

ELDON. Damn it, Jack! I never drank before. I don't drink now. I've never had no damn battle with any goddamn bottle. None of you know me.

FRANK. I think you'd better leave, Jack.

JACK. What the hell for? I don't have what's mine yet.

FRANK. We're going to bury Mom ourselves.

JACK. You are? Why?

FRANK. We know what type of funeral she wanted.

JACK. Then what kind is that Frank, huh? What kind?

FRANK. One that isn't bought and paid for. Doesn't come out from any showcase. She always wanted to be buried in the Indin way.

JACK. What do you think I would do? Put her in a pine box and leave her on the side of a hill, unburied?

FRANK. They don't do that any more – or do they?

JACK. You and your brothers are going to perform the funeral? You're the priest, he's the undertaker, and Kermit is the gravedigger?

FRANK. And if you notice, they're all family.

JACK. We have laws, health codes – state and federal. It isn't that simple.

FRANK. It was at one time. Just like dying was. Only you didn't have to pay anybody back then. And you had the time to say goodbye to the one you love. You didn't have to rush because the priest had an appointment, like a potluck. And our way means we don't have to worry about the price of a hearse or coffin, just the loss of the one we love.

JACK. You don't want your mom buried like the way white people do? And I'm so evil for that? You have to do better than that, Frank. A whole lot better. I've buried a lot of white people and your people in my days. They all have one thing in common – after a certain amount of time, they rot and they're forgotten.

FRANK. And I'm not going to let that happen.

JACK. But not with this body.

FRANK. You want a body, Jack? First, here. Here's some money.

> *(Takes some bills out of his pocket and gives them to* **JACK**.*)*

FRANK. This should take care of all the costs. And you want a body? Here. Take this one.

(*Pushes* **ELDON** *to* **JACK**.)

Or this one. Take this guy.

(*Pushes* **KERMIT**.)

KERMIT. Behave, Frank. Wok-ne-kit-due.

JACK. Oh, Christ.

FRANK. You want a body? Take one of these guys, or hell – take me. You're going to get one of us sooner or later.

JACK. All right, damn it. You had your fun. You tell me one thing. What is the mandate of heaven you have that the rest of us don't? You seem to have taken all the weight and secrets of the world on your shoulders.

(*He walks up to* **FRANK** *and puts the bills into* **FRANK**'s *pocket.*)

Go ahead.

FRANK. It's easy. When I say it, I mean it.

JACK. I'm getting tired and it's getting chillier. I'm thinking really seriously about getting the cops out here.

FRANK. You do that! You go ahead. I don't care what you do to us after the funeral. Just don't try to stop us from having it. I'm willing to sacrifice whatever I have to, Jack. Having this woman as a mother was a great gift. And now we're returning her back to her god, her family, her relations. We have an old woman to bury now, Jack. You can stay and watch or get into your car and drive off. It's a threat or an offer. Seriously – hey, it is serious – as serious as burying our mother. Now we have a funeral to start, Jack.

JACK. Frank, you can have your little funeral. Don't even bother to pay me. Listen to me – this is my threat, warning, or whatever the hell you want to call it. Don't you or your brothers ever cross me again. This is the last time and the first time it happens. I don't know if I can completely forget this. You guys sure the hell better hope I do.

(He begins to exit.)

I provide a service for people. You remember that. A service – and what they pay me for that service doesn't mean a thing. I do the work people can't. Enjoy your services.

(Exiting.) For Christ's sake.

ELDON. Good-bye, Jack.

*(Crosses to **FRANK**.)*

Do you think he'll call the cops?

FRANK. Wait.

ELDON. We sure the hell showed him though, huh? We'd better hurry up and start the funeral. If he tells the police, we won't have a chance.

FRANK. Wait a minute, El.

(Car engine starts.)

I'm going to be right back.

ELDON. You're not running out on us, are you?

FRANK. I said, I'll be right back.

*(**FRANK** exits.)*

ELDON. Pretty shaky ground, huh, Kermit? Kermit? Hey, Kermit. What's wrong with you?

KERMIT. You don't know what's wrong? Christ. It's what I did to Mom. I do all kinds of things, but I can never remember.

ELDON. Yeah. I know.

KERMIT. What's that?

(*Sound of truck leaving.*)

ELDON. That's Frank.

KERMIT. Well? You still mad at me?

ELDON. Do you really want to know? You know, Kermit, when you're sober, I don't mind having you around. When you're drunk, you can be a pain in the ass. You're the last person I want to have around me. Never knew anyone I wanted to hurt as much as you. Too much has happened.

KERMIT. What about Mom?

ELDON. What about her? I mean, she really worried about you. She always thought you might accidentally get run over, freeze to death, hit by a train. Something she just couldn't have helped. It happened to Uncle Joe.

KERMIT. He wasn't really our uncle.

ELDON. We claimed him.

KERMIT. Do you claim me? Tell me the truth?

ELDON. You're my brother through blood. I could disown you. I don't know any more.

KERMIT. Ach-noc-chew-luke.

ELDON. What the hell does that mean?

KERMIT. It's Klingon. You know? Your girls watch it. Live long and prosper.

ELDON. All this time, I thought...hey. Why don't you and I learn to speak Assiniboine? Instead of using this false language to speak with. We can find someone to help us.

KERMIT. Just you and me, huh? I don't know. What if I bring someone else with me?

ELDON. No. This is something we can do ourselves, or we don't do it.

(**FRANK** *enters.*)

FRANK. Ready?

(*He carries a sack.*)

KERMIT. Where'd you go?

FRANK. I used my pickup to block the road. Now no one can get in. Where's your quilt, El?

ELDON. Got it.

FRANK. You and Kermit roll Mom up in it.

(**ELDON** *spreads the blanket out.* **FRANK** *and* **KERMIT** *roll her up in it like rolling a cigarette.* **FRANK** *places more wood around the tree.*)

ELDON. Done.

FRANK. Now we'll put her in the tree. El, you take her shoulders – that end. Kermit, you take a stick and push back the branches when we put her in.

(*They place the body into the tree.* **FRANK** *sets the sack on top of their mother. He takes a braid of sweet grass from the back of his pocket.*)

KERMIT. Hey, what is that?

FRANK. Some tobacco and pemmican.

KERMIT. Oh, munchies.

FRANK. When I light this, we pray.

KERMIT. I hate to interrupt you, brother. Is there any special prayer we should say?

FRANK. Yeah. Your own.

> (*He lights the sweet grass. Makes circles around the* **BROTHERS** *and himself.*)

KERMIT. Now what, hey?

FRANK. I don't know. This is all I can remember.

ELDON. We should pray again, huh? The Lord's Prayer can be for Mom, as well as for white people.

FRANK. (*Awkwardly makes the sign of the cross.*) Our father, who are in heaven, hello it be they name. Thy kingdom come... thy kingdom come...

KERMIT. Does it have to be done.

FRANK. Does it have to done on earth as it is in heaven. Give us our day and our daily... our daily...

KERMIT. Daily fry bread.

FRANK. Daily fry bread. And forgive us our sins as we forgive those who have... those who have...

KERMIT. Those who have thrashed ass against us.

FRANK. Yeah. Those who have thrashed ass against us. Lead us not into temptation O lord, but deliver us from, from, from...

KERMIT. Lies.

FRANK. Lies. Thank you, Kermit.

> (**KERMIT** *farts.*)

FRANK & KERMIT. You're welcome.

ELDON. O heavenly father. These two men here are my brothers. We've come to bury our mother on this morning. She was a good woman. In all this world, you have given us a great gift: each other, and most importantly, this woman. We thank you.

KERMIT. Is this all?

FRANK. I guess it is. I've got some stuff to make some torches back at my truck. Let's go.

KERMIT. You guys go ahead. I want to think about some things.

FRANK. Sure. Come on, El.

> (**FRANK** *and* **ELDON** *exit.*)

KERMIT. Ob la di, ob la da, life goes on, la la la... Frank? Frank?

(To the body.) You're probably wondering why I called you here...

> *(He laughs, starts to walk away, and nearly trips.)*

Ma? Ma! Don't do this... please... I, I – I don't know what to do. I don't know. I thought I'd know what to do. Honest. I really did.

> *(Pause.)*

Ma?

(Softly to himself.) Mom, I ...

> *(He goes to where* **FRANK** *was standing, picks up the burning braid of sweet grass, tries to breathe in the smoke and then lets the braid drop.)*

Damn.

> *(He stands and looks at the body.)*

Ma, I don't know what to say. I always thought I'd know what to do when this time came. I know you've always been here for me. And now you're not here. Or are you?

KERMIT. You can't tell me what to do or say. I guess now
    I have to go on my own. I hope. Goddamn it, Mom!
    When you...left me...I could feel the tear. And no
    matter how much I drank, it kept ripping inside of me.
    And then it got cold. Cold all over inside of me. You
    know, huh? You know what I'm talking about? Like
    you with Dad? Forgive me, Mom. It's all I ask. Please.
    I want you to know. I was afraid I would drown you
    out with the booze, but I'm happy I didn't. I couldn't.
    I don't even know why I tried. We'll live long and
    prosper. Now what? What?

> (*He starts to hum a song.* **FRANK** *and* **ELDON**
> *enter carrying torches.* **KERMIT** *turns and
> waves them to join him. Without skipping
> a beat they join him, hold arms, and sing.
> Blackout.*)

www.ingramcontent.com/pod-product-compliance
Lightning Source LLC
Chambersburg PA
CBHW070420120726
47909CB00005B/1734